MONK CAMPS OUT

story and pictures by EMILY ARNOLD McCULLY

SCHOLASTIC INC.

New York Toronto London Auckland Sydney
Mexico City New Delhi Hong Kong

12 11 10 9 8 7 6 5 4 3 2   5 6 7 8 9/0   Printed in the U.S.A.   08   First Scholastic paperback printing, January 2001

Monk decided it was the perfect night for his first camp-out.

He'll be back
before we know it.

First, Monk had to make a tent.

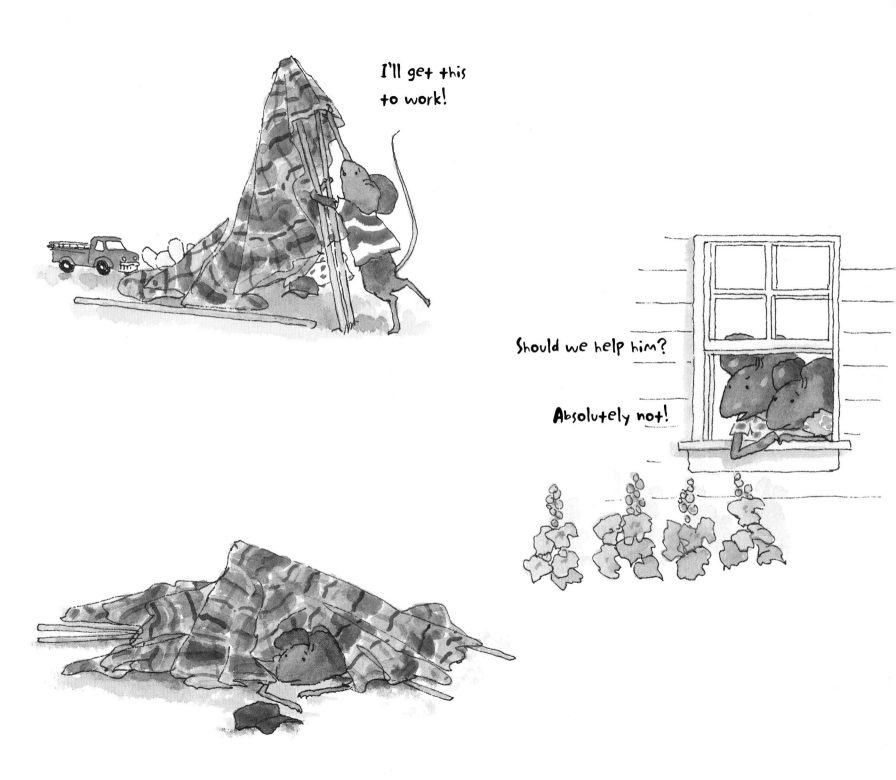

They only helped a little.

Of course, nobody answered.

Dinner was quiet.

The sun went down.
Monk watched shadows creep.
The kitchen light went out.
The living room light went on.

Who could sleep with all that quiet?

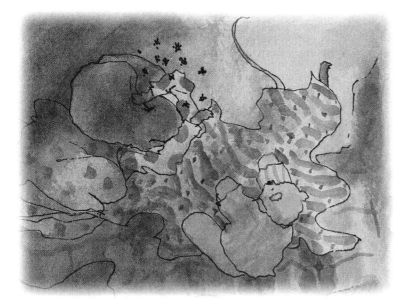 

The door flew open.

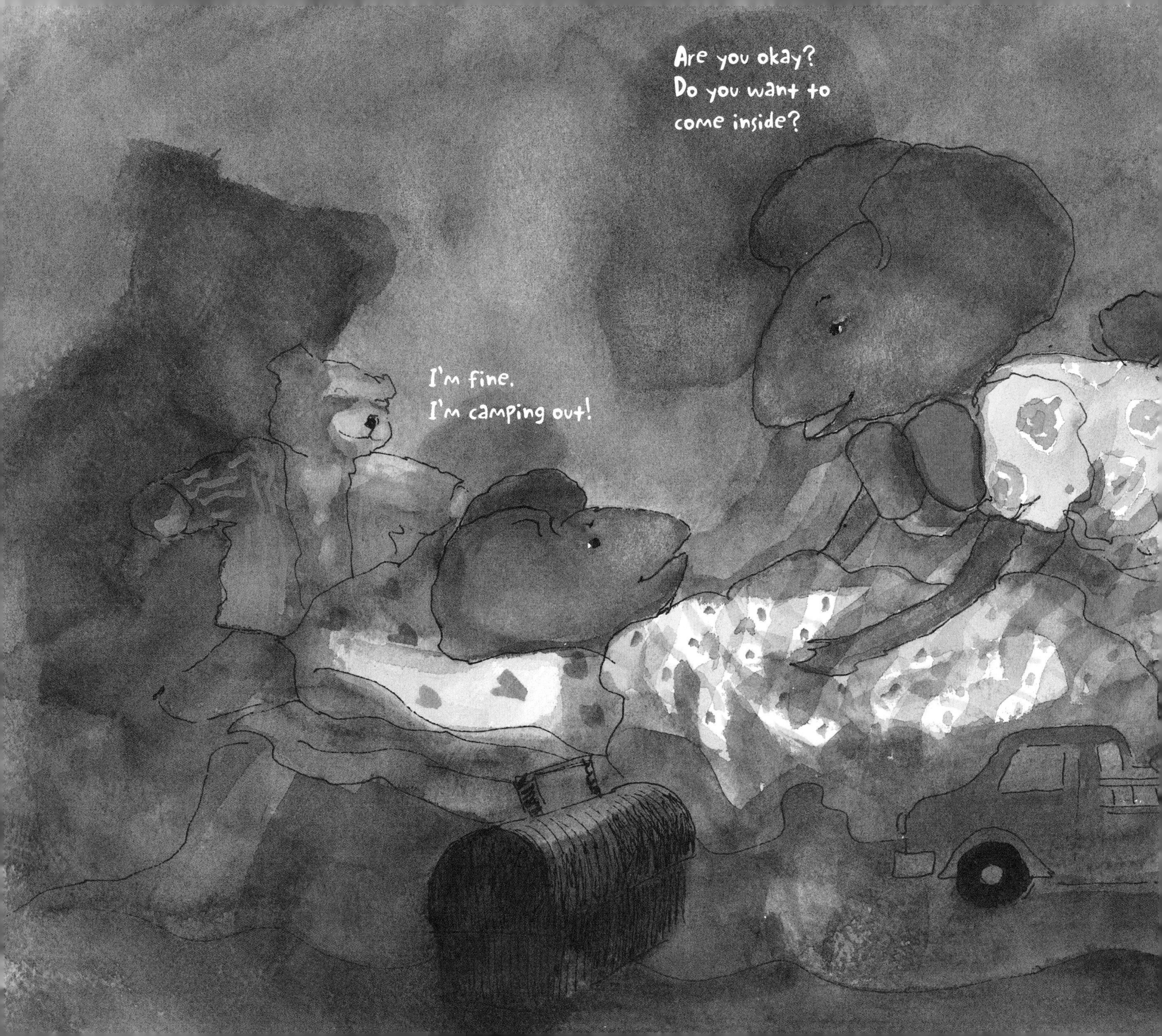
Are you okay?
Do you want to
come inside?
I'm fine.
I'm camping out!

They were proud of Monk.

He's very brave.

We'll just stay up until
he decides to come in.

Later that night, Monk woke up!

Where am I?

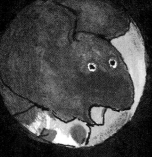

Where's my mitt?

Dad?

Quiet as mice, they peeked inside.

We'll just sleep out here and keep him company.

Mom? Dad? I'm home!
Where are you?

Mom's chair was still warm.

Good morning!

Where is everybody?

Zzzzzzz.